METABOLIZE, IF ABLE

METABOLIZE, IF ABLE

CLAY AD

MONSTER HOUSE PRESS BLOOMINGTON IND.

Metabolize, If Able — Clay AD

First Published by Monster House Press / Bloomington, Ind, 2018.

Second edition, 2019.

Novel • Science Fiction

© 2018 Clay AD

CATALOGING-IN PUBLICATION DATA

AD, Clay
[Novel] [United States]
[Germany] [Science Fiction]
Metabolize, If Able,
Clay AD, Pages cm—

ISBN • 978-0-9993985-1-7

Library of Congress Control Number: 2018939663

Book design & layout • Richard Wehrenberg
[richardwehrenberg.com]

Typeset • Bembo STD, Courier, Futura STD, Brandon Grotesque, Dosis, Frutiger LT STD, Arial, Lato

1 2 3 4 5 6 7 8 9 10 11

Arcadia Missa Publications
14-16 Brewer Street, First Floor
London
W1F 0SG
www.arcadiamissa.com

FOR MY FELLOW SICKOS

METABOLIZE, IF ABLE

I guess we were trying to infect the present, like have you heard of those bio-hacker collectives making homemade vaccines in their kitchens from specimens of super viruses collected from each other's fluids all mixed together? Anyway, I guess what I'm trying to say is that most days hold an endless repetition of unspoken terror, that life, in its daily, violently structured monotony, will never alter its frame. However, by making this film we stepped out of our given lives and refused to turn back. Wove our collectively inherited toxicity to make a representation of our rage.

The final scene has been called activism in some reviews, but we prefer to call it haptic-cinema made with the semiotics of revenge. Bio★Corp has simply called it terrorism.

Sometimes crisis is framed as an abrupt moment of reckoning, but for us it is clear it is always a chronic condition…

EXCERPT OF STATEMENT FROM RUBY PENNY ON HER FILM *TURN ILLNESS INTO WEAPON*

I was cast from a mold made from the body of a girl they found dead in a dumpster behind Bio★Corp.

DR LAD wouldn't show me her genetic code, the body, or even tell me her name. He said her name was found through face recognition software that traced her to an image online. The company never reported her death. If I knew her name, I would be a liability to the company, so like all other clones, I just call her, *prototype*.

He told me that everything about my genetics is the same as hers, except the manipulated fingerprints and eyeballs, which he designed himself.

Bodies, the dead ones especially, are a trade made between corporations to archive human DNA and thereby to create clones. This is not widely known information, especially to biohumans who distrust clones and actively avoid learning the histories behind our formation.

I am a clone and do not know specifically why they presently make and maintain clones, though I've gathered theories. It used to be the pharma companies investing in clone research. They planned to use our bodies as testing grounds for new medications and vaccines and even as incubators for organ transplants. This was not needed with the advent of specific biotechnology that effectively tested medication using DNA and genetic information from biohumans, because it could be done in a lab without testing subjects. We were made further redundant when factory farming techniques were developed for organs. Our bodies suddenly had no productive function. However, the corporate economies and physical structures of the cloning industry already had been instituted; it seems for the last few years they have experimented to find a new use value for their product.

The Corp augments our genetic code for auto-immunity, making us dependent on their medical care. We appear as what they imagine as healthy and able mind/body human specimens, but left to our own devices our bodies have a swift breakdown rate. Our maintenance program was developed as a replacement process. This means as we get ill to the point of life*collapse, entire bodily systems are replaced rather than mended or healed. Between replacements we are all compulsorily medicated to keep our system functioning and the pharma companies placated. Thus, cloning grew into one of the most viable and profitable industries for many economic sectors, vying to buy into our assumed product longevity.

As long as I am faithful to DR LAD (my assigned DR) and my Compulsory Wellness*Plan, I will always have guaranteed treatment. Biohumans are not so lucky. Because of the rapidly changing climate, toxic contexts and individualist attitudes, they are affected by rising cases of chronic illness, mutated viruses and environmentally based infections regularly, and only the very wealthy can afford care. Thus, most of them are in debt for a majority of their life or ill until death. Their body is collateral, and it is rumored that those who do not make payments end up in the dumpster.

One rumor on the clone and spawn forums is that Bio★Corp gets subsidies from the state for every clone formed because they are essentially a population control device. We are not fertile. If we did not spawn, our population would be self contained. It is also said that the amount of clones are all formed into subjects between the ages of 22-30, past this point older or younger ages are not represented. We do not age.

Economically, we are vital and can work as long as we regulate our health. We are strongly suggested careers by our DRs upon formation, and they help us to establish ourselves professionally through their connections; however, my concentration stats are so poor that DR LAD has given up trying to ease me into corporate environments. I work jobs that only last a few weeks or months—a short enough amount of time before my employer realizes I am not very good at whatever I am doing or that I'm too sick to come in often. This kind of living gets labeled as "unproductive," but many of us have devised alternative practices of surviving.

Yesterday I went to one of your movies bootlegged at the Dolly Theater.

The place is close to my apartment, built into an old convenience store. Two clones, Dex and Randy, moved in some years ago. Bought the boarded up store and then ripped its guts out to install six rows of seats, a screen, a little booth for the projector and a bathroom, all built out of found materials and scrap plywood; posters and notices layer and peel off the walls. The two sleep in the back behind the screen. Sometimes while the films are playing you can hear them bickering or fucking.

They sell moving images from before and also the current reels. The biggest crowds come for screenings of porn. The non-hetero clones and biohuman freaks, probably some spawns too. It's one of the few places in the city that clones and bios socialize, and there is not really anywhere else in the city that shows pre-Corp content. Technically, it's illegal as are the new reels bootlegged from the net a few days after the release in the Cine★Plex's. Since the Outers is far from the center and Corp jurisdiction, they're not too concerned, at least about copyright infringement happening at a little, clone-run theater. Local Corp security never do much of anything as far as public screenings and copy laws go anyway. They're more concerned about patrolling the net and feeds. However, it has become a locus of clone counterculture, so we're just waiting for the day it gets raided. We regularly de-bug the place, stay alert for undercover Corp people hanging around.

Dex likes to paint and recently he did the ceiling of the Dolly. He painted a group of animals from below. Some extinct, some still existent. I like to lie on the carpeted floor and look at their underbellies, paws and genitals; rabbits, cats, sheep, wolf, monkey, cow, mice, pigs…some of them look down towards the viewer and some off into the parallel plane they're depicted within.

The image is based off a famous photograph of a group of cloned mammals from many years ago. In the photo, they are shot face forward in a lab. In Dex's version, the sky is above them, light blue and clear, and between the animals are bugs, spiders, blades of grass, butterflies.

The same group of people usually show up to the theater. Tammy usually goes with me, but she was at inpatient getting her check up with Corp. We had pushed back the chairs and were all lying on the soft, stained carpet. Everyone cheered when you appeared; it was quite a way to see the film. In mixed company, my friends don't act like they know about you, but it was just us. It was nice there, everyone drinking and watching you on screen. Not scared that people will recognize and call out our likeness. Of course it's always strange to see your name written out "Starring: Ruby Penny…"

I'm not surprised that the plot line was upsetting. You did warn me.

CopyCat is a game Tammy and I usually play. Tammy always goes first:

My prototype was a poet. I have all these words that float through my head and I have no idea how they got there, I don't even know what most of them are! Things like: cherry blossom, synchronicity, moss, somatics, song bird, echinacea...

My prototype appeared more feminine than me, but had an aura of resilience that was intimidating to everyone that met her. She lifted weights and learned how to defend herself.

My prototype was a wild dancer at parties and a notorious heartbreaker. She brought people together! Let people hide out at her place, fed them and let them rest.

My prototype was in the middle of all the action. Remember that med heist that happened right before we were formed? That group liberated and redistributed meds from a warehouse outside the city. I think she was in that group, I just know it. That's probably why she got compromised and traded.

Don't flatter yourself! You don't come from those medi-Robin-Hoods. We're all out here trying to exist, remember? Your prototype was probably an unlucky biohuman who didn't pay her med bill to Corp.

Like most days, Tammy wakes up before me. Goes to the roof of our apartment building to tend to her plants and then comes back downstairs to wake me. We have our breakfast together in our sparse kitchen, at the old wooden table in comfortable silence: me drinking instant coffee and her tea, eating toast and powdered eggs. Recently she started writing poems since she got the idea that her prototype was a poet. I read the news off the forums. She never shows me those poems but says they are all about our *daily wonderful terrifying life.*

I've been living with her for a while now, though I only knew her for a short amount of time before I moved in. It's a small place—we share the same room and inside of our intimate domesticity we love one another—but our relationship is not particularly sexual. We have had sex in the past, but only when we were both drunk. Tammy mostly has a thing for younger clones anyway, *the fresh ones,* she calls them. I think it's because they're not quite as jaded post-formation. When we first met, Tammy was really into me for a few months; I was flattered but overwhelmed.

I was drawn to her intensity. Often for clones, "life" feels like an obsolete term, but Tammy is determined to live hers as hard as possible. She is obsessed with plants, specifically herbs, and using them to self-medicate and heal. She started when she found an old book about it, and then began wandering around the edges of the Outers, identifying and gathering seeds and starts between all the concrete. At this point she has even started to grow things for others' specific needs. One of the oldest clones I know, Diandra—she's at least nine years post-formation—suffered from terrible insomnia for a long time. Tammy began making her these teas and advising her on exercises to reduce anxiety, and now Diandra is sleeping more. A lot of clones now ask her suggestions for issues they're having.

Tammy's DR came on a house visit once because she had heard rumors of an unapproved healing transmitter in the Outers and knew about Tammy's gardening. She lied, said she was using them for cooking, threw some herbs into the sauce heating up in the pan on our dingy stove, saying *Look see here, this is all I am doing. Can you please leave now? I'm not your pet poodle you can watch while it shits, we deserve some privacy.* She got in trouble for that, but for weeks after we were calling each other 'poodle' fondly.

We met at a normalization training a few years ago, where we connected quickly. For compliant clones it's only required once a year, but for clones with low socialization stats it's required every few months or "as needed." Tammy has terrible stats. At one point, for a period, she would spit on her DR anytime she tried to come near Tammy. Through electrotherapy they broke her down. I wouldn't call her compliant now at all, she's one of the most anti-Corp clones I know, but she does pretend to play by their rules at least to survive. When she comes home from her DR appointments at Corp, she throws our stuff around the apartment and breaks dishes yelling, *fuck those fuckers white coat, shit heads*...until she collapses on the floor crying, breathing heavily and eventually falling asleep. I quietly go around after, picking up all the mess left in her wake. Push her meditation book across the floor with my foot to wherever she has collapsed, so she can read it when she wakes up.

SIMPLE AND DAILY GUIDED MEDITATIONS FOR FAILING BODIES IN PRECARIOUS STATES

By: Clone #85720

MEDITATION #1

The word *stasis* has two definitions, the first being *a period or state of inactivity or equilibrium*. And the second being, *civil strife*. In medicine, it is used to describe *a stoppage of body fluids*. In ancient Greece, it was used to report civil war, as in *the conflict named* stasis *was creating a stoppage within a region or organization as a means to alter or abolish the ruling system or class.*

How are your body's states of stillness and upheaval vital to one another? Think of trees; root systems; *rootedness*. "Rad" in latin means root; roots can be radical, destructive, medicinal, grounding us into place and earth. When are you unmoving yet catalyzing change?

I am sitting at Corp★Plex waiting for an appointment. I log into the Clone★Wellness System through my tablet to drop my location and to check in with DR LAD. He texts me that he is glad I am hanging out at ★Plex and that it is good for my socialization stats to be with other clones in Corp-approved settings.

My gut immediately tightens. I text back, *trying to be better. see you next week for our check-in!!! ;))))*

He doesn't like that I hang out and live in the Outers. It is a part of the city that doesn't have any Corp-approved structures or living centers, though there are rumors that eventually Corp will expand there. For now it is mostly full of abandoned buildings. Biohumans and spawns regularly get busted for biohacking and squatting buildings.

Compliant clones live and work close to the ★Plex in the center of the city. Upon formation I moved as far away as I could and soon found other outlying clones to live with. It's not good for his reputation in Corp to have a clone like me under his supervision, so every visit I get a lecture about the benefits of strictly adhering to my Wellness★Plan and the advantages of "clone2clone" socialization under DR supervision.

I wonder if the knowledge base I have is from the dead girl or if they uploaded random attributes from the net and created an algorithm for a personality. Trolled my prototype's feed and wrote an equation that self-generated the content she searched for. There must have been something about her though, something about Dex's or Randy's or Tammy's, or all the other clones that roll through the Dolly and don't give a damn about the dangers of us gathering like that. At least an energy or something. You can't completely erase all those people without some kind of ripple effect.

DR LAD
BIO*CORP
LOCATION: CORP*PLEX
CLONE: 39487
APPOINTMENT #3019

WELLNESS*PLAN

GENERAL QUESTIONNAIRE

DR QUESTIONS	BEHAVIOURAL NOTES	CLONE RESPONSES
How are you doing today?	Clone's posture is slumped and appearance is shabby. Pretends like they don't hear my question at first so I must repeat it.	Fine.
Do you have any pain?	Clone fidgets.	No more than usual.
How is your daily performance?	Clone looks at me as if I haven't asked this question before. Hesitates again.	Good.
Are you taking your medication as perscribed?	Clone looks me in the eye.	Yes.
Are you going to work?	Clone's gaze shifts back to their shoes.	Job ends in a week.
What will you do then?	Catch clone rolling their eyes briefly.	Go to the JOB*PLEX and register again.
Are your emotions still balanced?	Neutral expression.	Yes.
I don't like the clones you hang out with.	Direct gaze.	That's not a question.
I'm ordering you blood tests and a normalisation training to deal with your socialisation stats. That's not a question either.	Clone continues to look at me.	Can I go?

ORDER: - BLOOD TESTS, CHECK FOR VITAMIN AND MINERAL DEFICIENCIES, AS WELL AS WHITE BLOOD CELL COUNT
 - NORMALISATION TRAINING

FOLLOW UP: - JOB
 - EMOTIONAL BALANCE, I DON'T THINK MEDICATION IS CORRECTING DEPRESSION

I maintain my body by taking eight different pills everyday. Each is a unique shade of blue. Before I take them, I line them up in a gradient from light blue to dark. DR LAD says the pills keep my body's systems functioning.

Age is confusing. The girl they found was about twenty-five, I was told, so I tell people I am twenty four if they ask. I have been twenty four for a while now.

You are my liability; the company doesn't know I spawned you. Once DR LAD pointed to a picture of you in a magazine, next to an article on your new film. He said, *It's weird but she looks exactly like you, but more girly, like longer hair, you know?* & I laughed, sweating, *Wow that's so weird,* and quickly changed the subject.

If they found out I spawned you without reporting it, we'd both be compromised.

Statistically you shouldn't even be alive, spawning is supposedly a rare occurrence. Bio★Corp says there is only a .03% chance, but based on the chat history of the spawn forums it seems like a higher percentage.

I didn't know what was happening when you spawned, except the memory of the pain in my gut, unlike anything I had ever felt before. The fabric of my physical existence was breaking from the inside, and I could compare it to fire, but honestly metaphor doesn't suffice—it was pain, coming from all over my body, all at once.

I was on a bus heading to the next city, two hours away, to visit a friend from the forums when I felt the first signs. Before you made it out I ran down the aisle and slammed the door to the tiny bathroom, heaved into the toilet bowl, thinking I was going to be sick. I blacked out when you began to crawl out of my mouth a full grown adult. Saw the crowning of your head covered in blood and bile. Woke up on the bus bathroom floor, went to sit next to you, basically naked, except for my sweater clumsily pulled across your body. You looked up to me in a daze. We exchanged a few words. I told you my name, then got off at the next town and left you in the bus with a change of my clothes.

One clone wrote about spawning on a thread that they had spawned twice. I shudder at that thought. It's very painful, totally unpredictable and only happens when the clone is under extreme stress. Tammy meditates everyday, hoping it will never happen to her, compulsively takes rounds of herbal tea for the nervous system every few hours from bottles she carries around with her when we're out. Since I spawned you, she bossily leads me in breathing exercises every morning, squeezing my hand hard when I should breathe in and releasing on the breath out.

My decisions on the bus felt like the right thing to do at the time, but I wonder now why I left you there. After spawning I diagnosed myself with some kind of postpartum depression. Couldn't get out of bed for months. Only after I saw you in your first underground film a couple of years later at the Dolly was I able to find you again. In the shock of recognition, I quickly scribbled your name down from the credits and got a friend to find you on the forums.

who exactly r u?
Your clone, from the bus
...yr fucking w me
No its really me
where are u?
In the city
2 the north?
No the east, the outers
why r u contacting me?
I want to talk
u left me
I know...
...
I'm so sorry...
...
I regret it everyday
how did u find me?
I saw you in a film
my new 1?
Yes the new one
...
Can I write you? I'll explain everything ...
Please?
...
Please, let me explain
make sure its encryptd. heres the address...

sent: july 9 2030

hey- i'm glad you wrote. it's taken me awhile to know how to respond.

my bitterness towards you is like a blade. i hope it will dull eventually, but for the time being it's very sharp.

coming into the world with no point of reference was painful; those first months were the worst of my life. i try not to think of them. i've only recently gotten a grip on any kind of stability or reality.

my first day on earth i slept in a dumpster behind a strip mall. the first week i was so sick from shock i could barely move. the first time i had access to a tablet i researched "birth" only to find out i came out the wrong way.

i am happy you have contacted me, but seriously, fuck you. leaving me was complete cowardice. i'm scared that if i let you in you're going to leave again. i have a hard time trusting people generally, and so far you haven't given me much to work with. so, you better not become a ghost again. things are already too hard.
-ruby

The first time I met you in the flesh was about three years ago, shortly after we started corresponding. We sat at my kitchen table, drinking coffee and eating pie you brought over. Its filling was a vibrant red. Strawberries? Raspberries? I can't remember the taste, just the color. We talked quickly. We knew our being together was dangerous but that it was important to meet in real life. For me to explain my actions. For you to begin the long process of accepting those actions.

I remember something you said vividly, and those words stuck in my brain like the red did—

Hunger does not precede fullness. It is a life. I am empty though I act well; this is our commonality.

This memory of you catapults my mind to the moment when I saw you for the first time in a film. You are severely injured, your organs falling out. You are walking up a hill at night, to the top where you let loose a loud and long laugh to the dark night's stars.

Spawns like you are not on med lists, so you don't take eight pills a day. Your medical history is not legal or liable for coverage. Your organs are constantly failing in various ways, one after the other. When you go to the organ bank you pay in cash. Buy on sale. Add to your existing debt. Dodge the debt collectors who are rumoured to collect bodies if payment is not made. You hope the salary from your new film will make enough to cover your debts. You worry that your body will break at a rate more rapid than your rate of earning, leaving you either further in debt or dead.

A biohuman who lives in my neighborhood confronts me in the store. Tells me she saw me entering the Medi building at Corp. Tells me she knows I am a clone. They think we are corporate technology bent on a takeover. I want to tell her I did not ask for this. I want to tell her I was born out of death. I want to ask where is my agency to take over if I cannot function without their medicine every day? Instead, I quietly shake my head and keep walking. In my basket are oranges, a package of synthetic meat and a can of soda. Clone survival guides forgot to tell us how to breathe when biohumans are trying to out us.

My knee joints were in pain, so I walked slowly out of the store around the corner. Sat on the sidewalk to peel an orange and put the entire thing in my mouth. Didn't bother to separate the sections. Mouthing things in full feels better when I get the feeling: *I did not choose this.*

*Choice is a faulty concept as far as Wellness*Plans go*, DR LAD explains to me. I have many small daily options as a clone but little choice. *Clones are fortunate to come into a* *life planned out for them in many ways. We make adjustments accordingly to be sure. Without the stress of choice your immune system is stronger.* DR LAD concludes with a smile. *Now, on a scale of 1-10 please rate the amount of pain you're experiencing today...*

sent: december 17 2030

hey- the sound of cars pass outside and i'm looking out the window to a snow covered landscape. i have been staying in this house for a while now. i met patty on a spawn forum. she's helping me establish myself a little more. connecting me to people that make fake IDs and help us find work. i'm trying to think of a name that i like. did corp name you, or did you get to pick it yourself? funny i've never asked you that. patty found her name in an old magazine, biohumans think it's a tacky name, but then assume she's a weird biohuman. i've been using ruby as my name for acting so maybe i'll keep going with that. another person that lives here helped me get a job as a phone sex worker. i talk on the phone for about three hours a day. i have never had sex though, at least with another physical body. another spawn in the house told me that they would like to have sex with me sometime, but i declined. i copy erotica from the net to the people on the other line and listen to them getting off. mostly they tell me what they want to hear anyway and i'll parrot it back.

another friend here and i sit on the porch and he asks me questions about what i want. griffin is the first person to ask me that. he tells me spawns are special, and that, in a way, we get to have an unregulated relationship to desire separate from Corp, which seems to often control and normalize biohuman and clone desire. this he says is why we are the lucky ones. he speaks in a way i don't totally get. he's really into conspiracy theories, and when he begins on those i space out. i told him i wanted to be a famous actor, that i had already been in some underground films even. he grinned at that and said a spawn that was a celebrity right under their noses would be a big fuck-you to the cloning industry. he is very kind and very sick. he told me he doesn't think he will get better from this round of illness. we sit on the porch, him in his wheelchair and me on a swing hanging from the beam. we talk but also are together in silence while he smokes cigarettes and writes poems. i watch the steady stream of traffic pass in front of the house. the snow piled high on either side of the street.

patty's house is old, smelling faintly of mildew and body odor. it's decorated everywhere with potted plants and newspaper clippings about spawns taped to the walls haphazardly, certain names or portraits circled in pen. she has an open door policy for spawns in need of a place to crash, she is well known on the forums and people even joke her username should be *SurrogateMom_1*. she wakes up early every morning, even hungover, to make the house coffee and throw some cat food into the backyard for the strays that hang around.

i like these winter mornings because usually we're the only two that are awake so we'll sit and drink from chipped mugs together, both wrapped in blankets because the heat doesn't kick on until later in the day. patty tells me i should go have some fun, go out with her and her friends. patty sells illegal prescriptions, recreational and psychotropic drugs to biohumans, and hangs out at clubs to sell. i have never done drugs. i have been alive for such a short time i am learning the edges of my body and emotions, and *everything*, even the most boring things, seem new and i am devastated by how hard and sharp all these stupid things feel. the emotional and physical pain is braided together, so it's difficult to tell when i'm experiencing physical illness or emotional distress. they seem to come together as far as i have observed from my body's patterns. i tell patty i don't think i'm ready to do any drugs. patty says *it's cool, babe, no pressure*. she is able to maintain her body because she makes so much money from selling. she has her own unlicensed organ replacement technician and everything.

i also babysit a biohuman's baby who lives down the road. patty is the parents' dealer and she hooked me up with the job. i sit in their living room with the baby on my lap and put earmuffs over its tiny head and listen to their old music albums very loudly on the family's soundsystem. mostly the songs talk about love, which i don't really relate to, but it is good research for my acting. i think the baby can tell i'm not a biohuman. maybe that's irrational, but i have a feeling.

i have been reading on the forums about clones. do you know that the first clone was made psych-inpatient forever? she tried to bomb the biotech company where she was incubated. It was on the news about ten years ago. they hadn't made bugging or personal tablets for clones procedure yet so it was pretty easy for her to make a bomb unnoticed. DR LAD is probably terrified of you, terrified of my potential from within you. maybe i have talked to him on the phone, heard him coming in a weird croak. mostly it's wealthy biohuman men on the other line; the price is pretty steep, though I don't get paid all that well. not a big surprise, one fantasy i get asked to play out often is that of the DR/clone relationship. i always play the clone, the irony kills me. i'm close to you but far away. write back soon.-ruby

MEDITATION #2

We look to the body for inspiration: its ability to communicate across and with systems of incredible difference.

I went to see DR LAD recently. From the inside crease of my elbow they take eleven plastic vials of blood labeled with "CLONE #39487" and then my name. They have been looking for something. His voice keeps getting stuck in my head:

Fever?
No
Headaches?
No
Blood?
No
Diarrhea?
No
On a scale of 1-10, 10 being the most pain, where would you rate yourself?
A 2.

DR LAD smiled because he believes that he is keeping me from pain. I have stopped telling him the truth about my body, that there is a deep-seated knowledge that something is very wrong. Eventually he finds something in the blood work. *Your white blood cell count is low, we need to do tests, it's very serious. Come in on Tuesday morning. It could be lymphoma, radiation exposure or liver disease.*

I run my hand over the bruise inside my elbow.

Though you are not a product of Corp you have even less choice than I; there is increased rate of bodily failure, a possibility of termination if discovered, and an increased rate of stress because you must create a Wellness★Plan from scratch in a world bent on killing you.

In your latest box-office movie, I remember you coyly sipping through a straw on screen, the DR talking to you in a trendy, crowded bar and you listening to your love interest as the music swells. In this fiction you, the clone, overcome all odds and save the DR's life and then together discover the antidote to a super virus that is killing off biohumans. However, with careful observation of the film it is clear that all the complex character development is reserved for the DR. He is portrayed as a cold-on-the-outside caring-on-the-inside, cunning intellectual, with flowing sandy-colored hair, glasses and pale skin on the brink of translating a mysterious sequence of human genetic code. There is a moment when you nod your head slowly while he says, *It's not too late for humanity, there is still time for me to discover the cure.* And I swore it felt like you were looking past him, to me.

sent: october 5 2031

hey- everyday on set the feeling that I have no agency in this production multiplies. i'm slowly learning that the Director's even more controlling than i thought. i am eating a piece of toast with marmalade while i write this, drinking coffee spiked with whiskey and sitting on a stoop. i have so much pain in my gut. everything i eat hurts, i have stopped trying to avoid pain. it's hard to survive when it feels like your body has preemptively decided you're gonna slowly starve yourself. sometimes i feel like a babysitter for my own flesh suitcase whose parents totally left town and abandoned me to my own self-destructive devices.

a woman stopped to ask if i was who she thought i was, and i replied *yes, i am ruby penny...* and that i was in that movie. the woman asked for my autograph. all she had in her bag was a cheap romance novel so i signed the cover. my name now scrawled between some half-naked heterosexual couple embracing on a beach.

she asked me what i do for fun. i wanted to say *recently one can usually find me in my bathroom doubled over and throwing up.* but instead i said, *the cast all goes out after shoots together. we love dancing!* the sad thing is that is what i mostly do with my time when my body is able to fake it. i mean of course it's all for show, but the constant performing is really getting to me right now. last night i was out at a benefit for the producers, mostly corp people. i was charming and moving between them, conversation was easy. it's incredibly simple to convince people i'm fine, that i'm having fun, that i fit into their world. it's really just a game. one of the producers started hitting on me and offered me coke so we went to the bathroom. we'd snort some and between they'd ask me in a loud voice *HOW IS THE MOVIE GOING??? I LOVE THE DIRECTOR! SHE'S SOOO GREAT(!!!)* *she's great,* i answer. smile, snort, repeat, until i could make up an excuse to leave the stall. i'm glad i got high though, makes those things more bearable. it all becomes such a ruse.

just like this toast i'm eating is a ruse to make the passersby believe that there is an order to things, namely, a belief in the maintenance of the body. just as my fake ID is a ruse for my employers to believe that there is an order to things, namely, that this body was born in iowa in 2005.

though i know it's completely impossible, i imagine telling this woman the truth of my identity. seeing the look of horror when she realizes who i really am. i want to start making films again that do that: horrify people. confuse them. change them. anything except this placating shit i've been turning out.

like i can't stop imagining an ending to a movie where I burn the theater down. you are maybe the only person who knows the rage i contain costumed in composure: the ethics i have built around trying to eradicate fear by purging out everything, the sham i deeply believe i am, the desire i have to do something outside of my selfish world. it seems laughable that all i am doing right now is sitting on a stoop chewing this stupid toast slowly into a mush while waiting to go into makeup. all the while constructing a politics around a disembodied rage that could tear a movie screen into shreds, cooly walk away in sunglasses while the whole thing explodes and then get into a car and drive into the sunset. i guess this is what it feels like to sell out.

i'm embarrassed my only insurrectional activity is this correspondence with you, though for now i suppose it is enough, maybe more than enough when I think about it on good days. how much change can two failing bodies catalyze anyway? it seems like a rhetorical question, but i'm genuinely interested in your thoughts. please write back soon, everyone else is so boring. -ruby

MEDITATION #3

Pause to imagine the extrabiological objects in your life that facilitate meeting the needs and desires of your body. *(ex: the amino acid, tryptophan, which can only be obtained from certain foods and is processed through the digestive system. It is the precursor for serotonin, the neurotransmitter primarily responsible for feelings of well-being. Other examples: medication, water, oxygen.)*

Now think of how those objects that you ingest are directly connected to the state through production, control, accessibility and/or [a/e]ffect. How is your objective reality (those pills, that banana or the glass of water) coupled with governance and policy?

Recently we met on the ferry. It is my favourite meeting spot since it is beautiful, in constant motion and quite hard for anyone to overhear conversation. You wore a wide-brimmed hat to keep your face shadowed so we would not draw attention. I told you quite nervously that I had started to take testosterone. You were not surprised or judgmental, and for this I was grateful— you even joked that soon we could walk down the street together without as much concern of getting called for our likeness.

It feels like a quiet means of refuge. I am bargaining to make my body more livable under present circumstances. I went through the approval procedure at Corp for hormones and DR LAD was glad I had taken an interest in my Personal*Subjective*Development. Endocrine treatment for biohumans and spawns is nearly impossible to access, but for us within the Corp system it is quite easy. Some clones medically move between genders often. We talked about complicity; my body is changing and I like it. However, I feel ashamed that some things are easy for me. You said,

You are complicit, sure, but everyone is in varying degrees; we're "born" into these conditions, even spawns. The difference is what kind of care and work we put into building new scaffoldings of relation, even if for now they are secretly enacted only between us and a few others.

Before I spawned, my life felt like an illusion — veiled — some substance or material filtering my senses. There were cracks of light, sharp sensation, but mostly dull numbness. When you broke my body open, the veil fell away, and my eyes still have not adjusted. I am constantly navigating after images, hovering bright sparks that I take to be ghosts or floating lab coats or guardian angels from my peripheral vision. The feeling intuitively that you're always behind me. It's a kind of care. The undeniable reality that we are contingent even from afar.

DR LAD told me that a spawn in desperation came to him recently with a health emergency. The spawn couldn't afford an organ bank and needed a new lung, had tried everything, but finally decided to come to Corp as a last resort. The spawn could barely move from the pain. DR LAD agreed to allow the company to pay for a state-sanctioned lung and provide the surgery. DR LAD gave the spawn anesthesia and subsequently terminated them.

He finishes his story and begins pushing on my torso in different places. DR LAD says I need a new colon. Every time he pushes I feel a different pain.

We schedule the replacement procedure and then he hands me my prescription. I leave his office.

As the pharmacist hands my pill bottles to me they ask if I have any questions about the medication. I say *no, I have been taking these pills for years,* and they say *Sorry, honey, with y'all I can't tell who is fresh or who has been around for a while.*

sent: january 19 2032

hey- i don't have much of an update, just that i have been feeling quite blue lately. and lonely. taking some small pleasure in thinking about our last meeting on the ferry.

on the ferry your face was calm, but your voice quietly urgent. we caught up. i told you about how shooting was going and my mysterious symptoms and pain. you beginning hormones and the confusion it was causing. how Tammy was doing. Corp's goings-on. we moved onto other topics: the new health regulations for biohumans. more strict now, less coverage. autoimmune disease is common now even with biohumans. i was reading recently about how one scientist connected the statistics of autoimmunity to the toxicity levels in the ocean and that they have correlated for years.

inflammation is one result and symptom of most autoimmune disease. bodies are sometimes so literal. inflammation speaks through pain and discomfort; it is a refusal to conditions, diet, context, even to air. i have it too for sure. i haven't been to a doctor in months, but my gut feels like it's on fire. a spawn friend gives me a tip to only eat watery foods like oatmeal or soup so i've been trying that. i shit and shit until it seems like i will begin to turn inside out. ingesting soft things helps somewhat though.

we laughed about the wealthy biohumans who are obsessed with rejuvenation in the midst of all this. buying augmentations so they can live to be 150. who even knows what this place is going to be like in 20 years? on spawn forums we ruthlessly make fun of these people and their idea of life. in myself and the world i feel only the thinnest of lines between death and living. they must feel it too, fear it deeply. i guess i'm not as keen or as rich to stick around that long.

i got off the ferry first and stepped into the car waiting for me. you waited until the car pulled away and then went to the bus. that was the last time we saw each other in person, i hope to see you again soon, i miss you.-ruby

MEDITATION #4

Take note of the body.
Reconcile with discomfort as a state.
Metabolize, if able.
Repeat.

I play CopyCat with myself in bed today.

My prototype was deeply depressed. She couldn't get out of bed. She couldn't stop crying. She couldn't afford therapy or pills. She didn't have insurance. Her body hurt, and she didn't know why. She wondered if the depression catalyzed the physical pain or if the physical pain was inherent to the depression. She couldn't get up when she heard the protests or the riots. She watched the city falling apart on her tablet while her body was falling apart. She watched the coverage of the Dead Zones being emptied and quarantined. The checkpoints being instituted. The police violence. DRs making the first Corp clone. She couldn't get herself to pick up her tablet when her friends tried to call. She slept and only got up to eat. Some months she left the house, attended the meetings, took care of her friends, made some money, felt vital and even energized. But then something would shift, and she would go back to bed.

I call in sick to work. They know my status as a clone so they don't question my illness, but in a few weeks they fire me anyway.

When they let me go they say *You are not adequately performing at this job.* It is a job alphabetizing files in the center of the city. After they have fired me, I leave and unbutton my shirt to my undershirt as I walk out of the tall glass building and go back home to lay back down. I check into the Wellness★System and leave DR LAD a note that I have been fired.

He writes back *[angry emoji] this is the third time in the last two months. come in tomorrow for a counseling session.*

And then a few moments later *feel better.*

MEDITATION #5

Feel the realness of this day, different than other days. Your body in space.

Where and what you are leaving behind, and what you are moving towards—even when you are perfectly still?

Think about the small ways you declare your autonomy over your body daily.

Use the state of your bodily failure as leverage against the State.

Once, about a year ago during an appointment with DR LAD, I spotted four bottles of pills next to his desk on the cabinet. He left the room briefly to get something down the hall. I angled myself away from the door and security camera to quickly put one of the bottles into the waistband of my pants. He returned a moment later saying *So that's all for today, I'll see you in two weeks.*

On the door of his office is a wood plaque with golden lettering that reads *Do No Harm.*

The bottle was prescribed to another clone, #76093. Later Tammy and I looked up the drug, it was to increase concentration and productivity levels. We both took a double dose and stayed up through the night walking the boundary circle of the city. Passed by the cranes building towers in the center that laid empty, lit up with construction lighting, over the canal. Passed some graffiti on a wall that read, *turn illness into weapon.* Tammy whispered that she heard it was an anti-corp group's tag.

We were caught up in a hopeful energy, feeling like the city was full of an invisible potential. Talking fast the entire time, we built a fantasy that we would find an abandoned building, maybe an old hospital, outside the city and Tammy could open a clinic, we could open another Dolly. Tammy could grow her plants. The sun began to rise as we reached the outskirts where the fields and trees began. We turned around and started back home.

On the way back we passed a foreclosed organ bank with a sign pierced in the ground out front that read *FOR SALE*. The building's lights were on beyond the chain link fence that surrounded it and the parking lot. Tammy stopped to look at the building, an all-green glow. I came up beside her, our hands tightly holding the fence etching diamonds into our palms.

We turned at the sound of a voice. A man was loading a cooler full of human organs into his trunk in the parking lot. He yelled. Something about property. Something about get away. Something about w*hat the fuck are you two freaks doing?* He dropped the cooler and a lung hit the pavement.

Tammy and I both drew a sharp intake of breath and ran towards home.

The largest pharmaceutical manufacturer is in the middle of the country, an hour drive from here. Through the agricultural district, the wind farms, past two checkpoints. The pharma industry is an economic sector where the cost of research and development is very high whereas manufacturing costs are extremely low. However, product is sold based on the research costs and at an inflated rate. This makes acquiring drugs at cost impossible for all biohumans except the wealthy.

Despite this, DRs are eager to hand out prescriptions to clones. Clones are versed in the idea that if we are having a feeling with which we disagree, then it is chemical and individual and should be dealt with immediately to recalibrate our body's balance.

I wake up most days not wanting to be alive. I see this desire and hold it but do not feel the urgency to act.

I do not talk about this desire to DR LAD anymore. The first couple of months after formation I was still green to the system and told this feeling to DR LAD. He adjusted my pills, added a new capsule. For a few months I took this compliantly like the rest. It made me very distant to reality and I could no longer fall asleep. DRs of clones are not required by law to explain the drugs they prescribe to clones, though clones are required by law to take the pills prescribed. I did not like the side effects, so I told DR LAD the negative feeling had been neutralized and I felt no desire any longer to kill myself. I asked if my drugs could be adjusted. DR LAD said *No*.

Later I met up with Dex and Randy to tell them about this situation and asked if anything like that had ever happened with them. Dex took me to the back of the Dolly into their room and showed me a loose brick in the wall by his bed. He pulled it out and behind was full of pills. He laughed and said *Simple, just stick 'em in another hole!* They later explained that they kept the Dolly open by selling off their prescriptions to biohumans and spawns. I started doing this as well with the little capsule and suddenly had a source of income more reliable than my Corp-scheduled jobs.

At our Life★Orientation the DRs explain that if depression, suicidal thoughts, aggression, anxiety, panic, hallucinations, psychotic episodes, compulsive thoughts/ actions or any of the categorized "negative feelings or behaviors" are experienced, we are to report these to our DRs immediately and they will add the necessary drugs to our daily prescription to balance our stats.

I am not balanced. Balance is a myth. In DR LAD's office there is a chart of "negative feelings," which I have to rate from one to ten. The chart shows a cartoon face making a spectrum of expressions starting with a giant smile which leads at the end to a painfully crying frown.

I am forced to participate in auto-surveillance of my own body by pointing to the face I identify with the most every time I see my DR. I point to the one directly in the middle; it's mouth making a straight line, looking blankly forward.

sent: march 2 2032

hey- i am getting fed up on set, but there is nothing much i can do about it. i get fed up by fake acts of care. they feed us sandwiches, soda and trail mix. i pick out all the raisins and eat them slowly throughout the day so i don't pass out. i am fed up when the Director asks me *how are you, darling?* and then doesn't wait for my response.

i was interviewed for an article yesterday, they asked if i feel lucky to be a model to young people and had to do a double take to remember that my body presents a facade. you can't tell i'm spawn. can't read me at glance. the doubled-up luck of forgetting and remembering. no biohuman kid would want to grow up to be me if they really knew who i was.

i remember a couple of years ago right after i left patty's, before i got my break, and had only done a couple of small films, i was staying at a place called the "oasis motel" hitchhiking west. got picked up by a stranger who drove a truck and asked me if I wanted to make fifty dollars. i agreed and he pulled over. afterwards he took me to a tattoo parlor, told them to tattoo a zipper onto my back, told me it was so he could open me up. and i don't know why, but i got the tattoo. as the needle worked down my spine i felt dissociated from my body. it was a blank slate i could care less about. i woke up the next day with my back feeling like fire. terrified i ran out of the room to the gas station next door, scrawled a sign and stuck out my hand; continued west. got picked up by a christian family in a van who made me pray with them before letting me out at my stop, *lord please keep this girl safe and let her be guided by your heavenly light to a more righteous life, amen*. we held hands and when i slid out the door the mother handed me two sweaty ham sandwiches wrapped in plastic. when i got to the coast i got a job doing underground pharma-runs; for the biohumans with cancer, new viruses, mutated bugs, environmental things or wanting to get high. an easy way to make some money. this was when there were just a few checkpoints, so movement was a bit easier. sometimes i'd pick up a car full of medication and they'd all be sugar pills labeled as prescriptions.

one time a corp security car pulled me over out west and searched my car. told me he was gonna flag me for smuggling and distributing pharma-drugs, but he said *because I'm a nice guy...*and then minutes later i found myself sucking his cock. i didn't feel like i could say no. i didn't want him to run a background check on me and take me into a local *Plex, and anyway he could have forced me — we were in the middle of nowhere. i was still sitting in the driver's seat while he stood outside the door, his hips moving back and forth, blocking out the sun rhythmically over the desert. i felt like i was in a club, imagined staring straight into the strobe until i blacked out. he was holding my neck and choking me the entire time. he finished, told me i had ten minutes to drive away. later bruises bloomed where his hands had been. i only later realized what a fluke it was that i got away at all.

i was on a forum recently that was explaining how trauma is genetically inherited. basically meaning that the effects of extremely traumatic events and experiences are written into our dna and can be passed on through spawning or biobirth. when creating clones they attempted to remove any dna that had been affected by this from our prototypes but were unsuccessful. the dna kept making the epigenetic signals regardless of how much the DRs attempted to eliminate its presence. i guess there are some things that cannot be erased easily.

while i drove back east i listened to the changing landscape through the radio, bible belting, static popping, my own laughter. i loved this time alone in the car, though there was always the fear of getting found. in the confines of the car i made my own world. created elaborate plays where i acted out every character. built a story where lived reality was organized around care. dreamed in this reality i'd have my same body/mind but i would feel healthier just through a totally different context.

i stopped at the old house i use to live at years ago, all the spawns dead except for Patty. her skin looked strange, a little green and loose around her body. she took me in her arms. we laughed at the irony that now i was doing drug runs and she had started a much more demure stage of her life working part-time at a diner in the neighborhood.

that night i went to the diner Patty worked at. i sat at the booth to eat a sandwich and an older well dressed woman sat next to me. said she recognized me from my films. that was the Director. she told me about her new film and told me to come for an audition for it when i was back in the city. we were both drinking coffee and she was eating a plate of mashed potatoes, peas and some kind of synthetic meat. I was wearing a low cut shirt and she touched my back on my healed zipper tattoo telling me that i was even more stunning in person. my skin crawled but i was genuinely happy to have an audition lined up once i was in the city. now she brags that she liked me before i was well known, that she discovered me in middle america at a diner. this narrative satisfies her. she also told me once at a party drunk, leaning in close to my ear that she had a photo of me from that film where i played a witch. she confessed she has a thing for those who look half dead yet radicalized. she told me that she would masturbate to that photo but took it down, because her boyfriend thought it was weird and got jealous. *look at us now!* she would exclaim and grab my arm tight, laughing loud at parties with producers, *we're as close as a couple of clams!*

after talking for a couple of hours in the diner that day she took me out to her car, drove me to an abandoned strip mall parking lot, and we fucked in daylight. it was winter so we kept on all our clothes, even our jackets.

we've kept this arrangement going, and though it's not on my contract i know my employment is dependent. when we are alone she calls me *darling*. when we're in public she calls me *my star*.

i have too much time to think right now. my head is going through the past in images quickly like an old film reel. i look at the zipper tattoo in the mirror now and can't even relate to the person who let someone do that to her, but it's simultaneously a part of my body now that i intimately know and accept as much as my limbs, lungs or fingers. anyway, let's make sure to see each other soon. i keep thinking about your idea for the film you wrote me about. i can probably find someone to write the screenplay. it seems like forever since i've acted in something i actually care about. making that would certainly change things.-ruby

That first time I saw you on screen, you played a witch who was tortured for performing healing acts. Though they turned her body inside out as her punishment, she continued to live life in the village, all of her guts dragging along around her. The other villagers quickly accepted this as normal and began going to the newly implemented degree-holding DR for treatment. After a while they even began to forget who the woman was at all and just called her "crazy."

Your crimes consisted of: living alone, refusing to work for the lord or call yourself his vessel, having multiple lovers, knowing the name and uses of wild and cultivated herbs, minerals and trees, performing abortions, overseeing births, defending common land, cursing rapists, training and spreading your knowledge to others. The film was made by a group of artists and, after its release on the feeds, was immediately banned.

The screenwriter was arrested for libel. The rest of the cast and crew were required to attend a normalization training. That was a couple of years ago though, policy has gotten stricter.

In the waiting room at the Medi building we are required to fill out a form asking different questions such as *Have you been angry/irritable/edgy lately? Have you been energized/elated/high/out of control lately? Have you been discouraged/depressed/low/blue lately? When you wake up in the morning are you happy with your life? Have you ever thought of doing away with yourself? If so, how? What would happen after you were dead? Do things seem unnatural/unreal to you? Do you ever feel detached or different from others around you? Are there thoughts or images that you have a really difficult time getting out of your head? If you were in a movie theater and smelled smoke, what would you do?*

When I first told DR LAD that I thought about suicide sometimes he asked *Why would you want to kill yourself? You are a clone. You have a chance to start building your life free of many things. You're free from the trauma of childhood. Free of medical expenses. You have DRs watching over you. You are free.*

And I wanted to answer *Of course I want to. I was cast from the body of a dead girl.*

MEDITATION #6

Embody your conception of the term, *bioperversity*.

sent: november 27 2032

hey- this might come as a surprise, but i am experiencing momentary fullness. i am allowing myself fleeting feelings, allowing some food to stay down (though i still can't keep on any weight). i'm playing the lead character in this film and simultaneously falling for someone during the shoot. ree is their name. they are one of the people working the camera. they are quiet, but we get along well. after shoots we go to their apartment and hang out. i don't let myself get connected to biohumans often, but with ree it feels easy. we make fun of the other actors, make faces during work and roll our eyes. they are full of anger as well. we watch the news and spit together at the idiots opening and closing their mouths. we lay on their floor and listen to music, laugh at the stupidest things for hours. they read me film scripts they've written. the scripts are great, complicated and messy, and they'll probably never get made.

ree complains they know nothing about me. i have told them all my anecdotes about my made-up life. the boyfriend i supposedly had in college. the college i supposedly went to. the parents from whom i have supposedly estranged myself, and about whom i'm supposedly bitter. my childhood, shown in stock photos minus the watermark. they can sniff out the flatness of my story. i do tell them about you; not how we know each other, but just about you. i tell them you're my best friend, basically family, they want to meet you. i know that's impossible; they would stop, look from my face to yours. and then we'd have to...kill them? i trust them, but when you and i are together our biolinked narrative is too obvious. but regardless of the danger, it's nice to let someone in, even a little bit. i told ree about your idea for the movie. ree wants to help us write the script. if it can come together quickly i can even get some people together to shoot it soon, some of my old underground film friends maybe. we'll see if they will pick up my calls, i haven't been the most responsive in the past couple of years.

yesterday ree and i walked through the park back to their house at night. we took a path i didn't know and found an old arched bridge with a body of water underneath. we didn't understand where we were at all. they pressed me against the old stonework and kissed me. their touch is comforting to the point of pain, but not the pain i know. the pain of something nice slowly rooting itself around all my gross insides. i feel scared and already ruined. they leave little scratches and bruises on me that i treasure and look at for days, though they are considerate and always avoid the skin that will show on camera.

my performance in this film is going fairly well because i'm transferring all of this confusing emotion into the character i'm portraying. i am feeling changed, though i don't think it is very likely this relationship can go anywhere. it's making me feel possible in a way that felt foreclosed, previously nonexistent. the opening up is deeply uncomfortable, my doors creak and are rusty.

i'm trying hard these days to be a less nihilistic person. this feeling is a moving landmass, i mean tectonically i get it, but it's changing the cartography of my understanding. previously i have only known violence and alienation in connection to most human relation. how do you amend years of landscaped desire bent on beating you back into yourself before you started to extend?

i could go on, but i feel cheesy. it is nice, though, to have a someone to take my mind off of all the bullshit. it would be nice if you two could meet someday. -ruby

My body is a text—genetic code edited and proofread by the DRs.

However, in the night, with friends, in correspondence with you, I am slowly redrafting. Small things change. I am growing traces of hair on my face. You're hatching plans. Hazy horizon lines appear in our distance.

At the Dolly, I get high and feel held as we all lay around coming down while Dex screens banned films. I sing under my breath while I walk to Corp for my check up. I let Tammy push her homemade medicine on me. I let myself sleep when I feel pain. I reckon and even enjoy life inside the misread.

I met up with Tammy in a cafe before a party was set to happen. We drank some tea and then headed over to Bee's basement apartment together. There was music playing from a rewired tablet to an old radio. Though the room was dim, it was lit enough to see clusters of bodies dancing, and beneath the noise clones gathered by the walls to talk in whispers—about recent spawnings, corp news or disappeared clones. Tammy immediately started making out on the couch with a clone who was new, only half a year post-formation. Randy and I grinned and rolled our eyes at one another.

I left the group to walk around, said hello to a few people and worked on my drink. That night I felt surprisingly present and with less pain. The dance floor was crowded. I registered how many people were in the room. It was the largest gathering of those whom I'm assuming are fairly non-compliant clones, that I had ever seen together. The host, Bee, is well known and notoriously anti-Corp. She made a pamphlet a few years ago that she handed out at normalization training called "*De-normalizing Your Brain*: How Your Body May Be a Corp Product but Your

Thoughts Don't Have to Be." That really pissed off the DRs, one of them with a tight-lipped smile held it up asking *Now who made this...Come on, please come forward. Now don't be afraid to come forward we would love to talk to you about the ideas in it.* No one said anything, but later we were all strip-searched by security, and the pamphlets were confiscated.

I came into the kitchen and sat on the counter. Bee came in just as I was thinking of her and began to show me these stickers. They read *Turn Illness Into Weapon.* Someone has been scrawling that same phrase all around town as well. *You want some? I've been sticking them everywhere. The slogan is from some pre-Corp patient's collective. A group called Malady has been putting it up everywhere, it sounds nice, right?* I agreed and took a few of them. We continued to talk for a long time, Bee kept refilling my drink whenever I got to the bottom of the cup. As I got more drunk, I explained the plot line of our screenplay idea to her and our tentative plan for its release. She listened intently until I finished, went to her room quickly and came back with a folded-up paper that she handed to me. On a blank sheet she wrote down some names and numbers.

This, she whispered urgently while gesturing to the folded paper, *marks where all the known checkpoints are, it's a map. When you get home, copy it and then bring me back the original as soon as possible. When you're not home, hide the copy somewhere safe in the house.*

Yeah, of course. Who are these people?

Malady. Don't go getting in touch with them until right before you need to. They'll be excited about Ruby Penny. Her involvement in the movement or the fact that she is spawn can be used very strategically against Corp. Her eyes darted back to the paper in my hand. *Good to memorize their information, less trace the better.*

Randy wandered in, and I shoved the papers into my boot. He was a drunk and started telling me about how Dex thought someone else was cute and how that was making him jealous. Bee gave me a heavy smile then went back into the main room of the party.

MEDITATION #7

Durational experiment:

See how long you can go before your body breaks in a truly exceptional way.

Exceptional enough that your DR will pathologize it.

Exceptional enough for them to name the failure after you.

Exceptional enough that at the end there is an *aw* and applause, not for the life lived but for what took you out of it.

I come in and DR LAD has three assistants around him. They begin to take my temperature, my blood pressure and my pulse, all at once, grabbing at different parts of my body. I am conflicted, because I am accustomed to their use of my body without consent, but, regardless of their standard behavior, it still terrifies me. I dissociate and then come back when he asks me:

Any blood in your stool?
No
Chills?
No
Are you taking your medicine?
Yes
Fever?...

DR LAD has been very concerned by how much weight I'm losing recently.

DR LAD says my medication is not showing up in my blood tests *Are you taking it?* He asks me again.

Yes I answer.

That's what I thought. Maybe your system isn't responding to the medication anymore. I'll order some more tests, maybe you need a new kidney. . . or pancreas. . . or liver. Hell, maybe we should do an entire new replacement, you're due for one in about a year anyway… Let's take some blood.

I go home, remove my afternoon dosage of medication, walk across the room into the bathroom and then gently press my hand on a loose tile. I slip my hand under and add the dose to a plastic bag full of pills.

I go onto a forum for clones who are self-terminating. Self-termination is a method of slowly decreasing dosage until medication is not taken. The medication is saved and sold illegally or given to spawns. Some clones just do this in bursts, not long enough to result in total bodily collapse or to show up in tests. It is risky though because sometimes once medication is reintroduced it might not work as well—or at all.

Bruises shadow the inner elbow, barely enough time between drawings for the bruise to fade. I imagine myself as just a shadow without a body, a bruise that sits opposite the sun.

The bag full of pills is for you.

MEDITATION #8

Sharing pain involves trust with another
The communication of pain involves belief*
When an experience of pain is doubted
The subject begins to question their
Somatic experience of embodied knowledge

Once doubt (either from an external or internal force) has been introduced it appears as a feedback cycle rotating through:

1. The subject's mistrust in their own body's interpretation of the named "pain"
2. The subject concluding they must be mad/crazy/attention seeking for inventing the state of pain
3. During this time subject continues to actually experience the felt reality of the pain (cycle goes back to 1)

*i.e. listening, mutual aid, reliance, a stake in another's communication of the body's experience through language, viewing the body as a holistic interconnected system(s), recognition and admittance of the relationship between trauma and pain; context and pain; identity and pain, then reiterating to one another as often as needed that: *you are not crazy/the world is crazy.*

I come home to Tammy drawing. She is making a map. *It's my own Wellness*Plan. You should make one too.* She hangs it in our kitchen over the table.

Sometimes when my body hurts I yell in pain or whimper. However, usually I quietly listen to the roar of the great big ocean that wants to tear me open from the inside. I imagine cutting a small hole into myself and out comes a geyser, a mass of moving water bigger than my body.

The only sexual relationship in my life right now is with my friend Astrid who is a professional dominatrix. We meet at their apartment and have our sessions in their room which is impeccably clean. They're also a clone. And that, I think, gives them an understanding of the complexity of pain and its nuances. Our safeword is *shine*.

I get hit repeatedly until I can quiet my brain; this pain is predictable. This pain I have asked for, understand, ingest and enjoy. Here, on my stomach, while asking for *more*, I recede into myself and play CopyCat.

My prototype lost her lover in one of the epidemics. She also caught the virus but survived. After the funeral she came back to their home and burnt it down for the insurance money. It barely paid for any of the hospital bills that had accrued between them both. When she left she only took the truck they had shared and a needlepoint her lover had made, which read, "Bless This Mess."

I am shaken from my game as Astrid hits me hard across the back and commands *Be present, clone.*

sent: april 10 2033

hey- i am writing you from the last few days of shooting. the Director wouldn't tell us where we were, though clearly we were in a dead zone. these old empty cities are perfect for movie shoots, the crew can fill up the space with exactly the ambiance they want and not have to worry about civilians walking through the shoot. it's creepy to me though. we can't even be here for more than a few days because of the chemical levels. i've gotten this weird cough from breathing the air here.

i won't even be able to send this until we're back in the city and i can access the forums. i have complicated news. i heard through techcrew gossip (ree) that the Director knows i'm spawn. i guess a lot of people do now, and the scariest part is that i don't know how they found out. i'm so compromised it's not funny, and i'm worried you could be too. apparently the Director threatened everyone to keep quiet about it. she believes this film is going to make her career... ree thinks she will blackmail me with a lifetime contract after this film... i wouldn't put it past her, and i will just have to agree. if she does tell corp of my existence i'm dead. i read on the forums that sometimes they keep the spawns for lifetime blood banking. but i can't imagine they would take me being alive very well, i'm too well known by biohumans. for now i'm feigning obliviousness. i don't know what to do. honestly the idea of being wedded to her for even one more film makes me sicker than i already am. i want to quit this. i cannot make another film. i'm in pain, though i constantly am needing to act and fictionalize my health. my character is young and in love with a DR. she is a few years in the past in one of the old cities. she approaches conflict with a level head. she says the right thing at the right time. it's almost fun to pretend to be her because it feels like such a far off reality.

at night ree sneaks into my trailer and it's then that i guess i am most myself right now (though an examination of the phrase "most myself" is laughable... which self? i guess i feel nearest to myself with you and that is closest to a truth.) ree cooks me food so i eat, usually we cook some synthmeat and potatoes, get drunk and fuck.

in down time around the shoot i walk through the city and pick up bits of things from when this city had people living here. signs with funny letters, broken lighters, even a long red acrylic fingernail and a carbon-copy pad! do you know what carbon copies are? maybe only from a movie or something, but the premise is that you write into it and the carbon copies on the paper behind it. it reminds me of us, a copy of a copy...of another copy. me to you to our prototype. writing and pressing into each other endlessly...

on the shoot today i willed myself to read the final scene of the film. i die. i let out a laugh and sat on the ground. the others at the shoot looked at me funny.

she sacrifices her herself to test an antivirus before giving it to the DR. it kills her so he knows it is faulty. he makes the adjustment and then injects himself and lives. it's a ridiculous idea that i would kill myself for a man or biohuman at that. i know the only way i will kill myself is to avoid being taken by corp. i have a stash of pills i carry with me for the occasion. now that they know i'm spawn i tell these things to ree and they tell me to stop being dramatic. but they've slowly started to get it—recently we found out how much my transplant is going to cost. the money from this movie is barely going to cover it. they've looked at me with scared eyes these last days, hugging me tight. it's nice but strange now that they know. i feel exposed with them in a way I only feel with you. i asked on a spawn forum if anyone else had ever dated a biohuman. the responses were interesting. some were very against it, said it was too difficult, the difference of experience too vast and the spawn would always be the in the position to be mistreated. others said only if it was a means of survival. biohuman sugar daddies and mommies…a handful talked about how they had found an understanding biohuman. one told a story about how their partner was a biohuman with the same blood type and would donate to the spawn regularly during transplants. they described being directly hooked up to one another with an IV tube. it sounded kinda hot.

anyway, this whole rambling mess is to say that i'm mailing you a copy of the film soon. i think it's about time we actually do this. the gig is definitely up. there is not much more left to lose if the truth of my spawn status is already on the table. i'll send the file your way soon and we can decide a date. love -ruby

I want the antidote to my condition. I want it to be that easy. I want it to be a single pill left in a jewelry box on my doorstep. Cures are never that simple though, never unbiased, nor so individualized, rarely that romantic, and to be honest, I don't believe they exist. A myth that brings more hurt.

Regardless, I know it's naïve, but for a minute I'd like to imagine it's possible.

Your film came today, delivered by a spawn. We watched it at the Dolly. Everyone cried at the ending, said it was the best thing they'd seen you in. Dex is getting someone to help us with the hack but told me our plan was risky. Tammy isn't talking to me, I even told her she should come with us. She just keeps reading her mediation book, furiously scrawling poems and ignoring me.

If it all goes well, the film will play across every feed on the same day your new Corp movie is set to release.

(what is it?) (*I am worried this won't work.*) (me too, but everything will be okay) (*What happens when the underdogs win?*) (in the movies?) (*Yes.*) (they get away) (. . .) (we'll get away, we'll figure it out.) (. . .) (i will be there to pick you up) (*Is ree coming too?*) (yes, we're all implicated at this point, them as much as you and me) (*I want to go.*) (i know) (*I've been feeling so sick lately, it's hard to get out of bed.*) (we'll figure it out) (*I have the pills for you, I want out of this, I want to go through with the plan on my side. I'm frustrated.*) (when we leave we can fix our bodies, i have a contact with a replacement technician down south who does pro bono work for people in the movement. we can even have a co-operation, with tables side-by-side if you want.) (*I think the real issue is I cannot imagine myself out of this crisis, outside of Corp control... my mind goes blank and I feel like I'm falling off a cliff. I feel like I'll just die.*) (that is what happens when you refuse the future they augment you with, you have to learn how to imagine other possibilities) (. . .) (that's what spawns learn at least, we have to aggressively write ourselves and our bodies and desires into the world because nobody will do it for us)(*I know, but I'm worried. what happens after we do it?*

Where will we go? Bee gave me that map and those names, but I don't know if that's enough.) (once you go to Corp and start the fire, i'll be waiting outside for you. i have contacts, it's going to be okay)

I wake up unable to move. Today is the action. Tammy comes into my room, looks at me and says *Wow, you look fucking awful*. Then pauses before asking *Where's the stuff?*

It feels difficult to speak so I point to the canvas bag beside the bed. It contains a gallon of gasoline, a bag of homemade thermite, a lighter, my pills and the few possessions I planned on taking with me. She picks it up.

I'll do it. I think this is a shit plan, but I'll do it. I'm coming home after though. I'm not leaving my plants. We're putting those in the car with us. Tell Ruby to make room for them. I don't care if we have to throw her biolover out of the car.

She quickly puts on a wig and sunglasses, expertly paints on some makeup and pulls a hoodie over her head. She picks up the canvas bag and hugs me. I kiss her on the cheek.

See you soon love.

The film interrupts the feeds at 8 o'clock in the evening as planned. I am in bed with my face close to my tablet watching our work. I drift asleep before the ending and wake to Tammy violently shaking me.

MEDITATION #9

Imagine your most ideal life playing as a movie. Are you watching from inside your body? Are you watching yourself from outside your body? Is the point of view from your eyeballs? Your gut? Your hands? Do you have a body? Are you human? Do you look different? Do you feel different? Is there a lot of dialogue? Is it a silent film? Are you the same gender? How is your health portrayed? How does your body function? What is the lighting like? What are you able and unable to do? What kind of power-dynamics exist? Who takes care of you? Who do you take care of? What is your living situation like? Do you live alone? With other people? What is your love life like? How do you survive and meet your needs? What are your needs? Desires? How is the footage edited? Are there fades, jump cuts, montages? What is your relationship to money? Does money even exist? How does community function? Does the camera always follow you, or does it focus on others too? Do you enjoy the same activities? Are you the same age? Older? Younger? What is your environment like? Do you find yourself inside? Outside? Underground? What is your social life like? Who wrote the soundtrack? Do you share your secrets? Are you open? Vulnerable? Mysterious? Funny? Traumatized? Is it subtitled? Is it subtle? Dramatic? Slapstick? Horror? Drag? What are your politics? How do you express your politics? Is it an option to express your politics openly? Do you make plans, or go with the flow? Do you have a pet? Do you have a plant? Do you listen to music? What is your relationship to the land? What are your close relations like? Do you have family? Are you close to your family? Did you have to make your own family? Do you have friends? Are you a loner? Was it shot on a GoPro? A phone? 16mm? Is it HD? Was there a film crew? Did they get paid? Did you get paid? Did you get the rights, or did you sign away your story?

Imagine you're in the theater watching this movie about your life. You smell smoke. *What do you do?*

Turn Illness Into Weapon

Screenplay by Ruby Penny and Ree M.

NOTES

"Turn Illness Into A Weapon" is the title of a communique from the Socialist Patients Collective (Sozialistisches Patientenkollektiv, or SPK) founded in Heidelberg Germany in 1970. SPK questioned the patient/doctor paradigm and ultimately called for an overthrow of the "doctor's class." They argued that the sick were inherently insurrectionary to capitalism through their inability to be productive, "functional" subjects.

The character JANE is named after the Jane Collective in Chicago, Illinois which existed from 1969 to 1973. The group illegally provided abortions to women before the passing of *Roe v. Wade*.

PRIMA is named after the first clone created by Corp ten years ago.

FADE IN

CANAL RUNNING THROUGH INDUSTRIAL MIDWEST CITY-
TWILIGHT

A handheld camera follows ASH, who is walking down the canal that runs across the city's center. She is in her mid-thirties, with a buzz cut, dressed in canvas pants and shirt. There is a shot of her face, which is expressive, smiles easily but also shows a deep tiredness under her eyes. She is carrying herself with confidence, though periodically looks around nervously as if lost. She comes to a stop in front of an unmarked building and enters down a hallway to a door painted with a small green spiral. She pushes open the door and enters.

MEETING ROOM-NO WINDOWS, LIGHT FROM A SINGLE BRIGHT LIGHT BULB

The room is surrounded by shelves on all sides with pill bottles, herbs, books and medical supplies, which the camera pans randomly slowing to create vignettes of objects. There are posters and photos on the walls; the room looks well used and messy. The camera cuts to a long shot of a group of about fifteen people sitting in a circle in the middle of the room talking intensely, one person translating the conversation into sign language. Some sit in chairs, some in wheelchairs, some on the floor. The conversation stops abruptly when ASH walks in. They all turn towards her. She takes a seat.

                    ASH
Sorry I'm late, I got a bit
lost.

                  LORRAINE
It's all right, we're just
starting. Can you introduce
yourself and let us know how you
found out about the meeting?

                    ASH
A friend of Jane's told me about
it, is Jane here?

                    JANE
I'm Jane. Which friend?

                    ASH
Mars, I met him at the bar by my
house, he said you were looking
for new members.

                    JANE
Okay, yeah, Mars said he was
sending us someone.

                    ASH
(Looks around and laughs
nervously)
So, yes that's me. My name is
Ash, and I just moved to the city
from about an hour south of here.
I was a part of a pretty small
group doing anti-Corp work in my
town, and so I'm here to continue

that hopefully and find some kind of support system as well.

                    MAX
Thanks, we're glad you're here. We usually ask new people to listen for their first meeting. As I'm sure you know, everything that's spoken stays in this room.

                    ASH
Of course.

                    MAX
You didn't bring a tablet or anything did you?

                    ASH
No.

                    MAX
Okay, let's get back to it.

The meeting continues and Ash stays silent.

CUT TO MEETING ROOM-LATER

The meeting is finished and people continue to mill about in the room. Someone makes tea, some are holding beer cans circled in conversation, one person gives another acupuncture in the corner, another person is cataloging shelves of medication. ASH is standing alone and then is approached by JANE and WINNIE. JANE is in her early 20's, wearing jeans, lipstick and glasses. WINNIE is an older woman in her 50's with long white hair down her back; dressed in white cowboy boots, a grey button down and trousers walking with a cane with a crystal handle. Her aura is intimidating but warm. ASH'S attention fully turns to WINNIE.

JANE

What do you think?

ASH

(Turns focus back to JANE)
The group's actions are more... extreme than I'm used to, but that is what I've been looking for I think. I'll definitely keep coming, although I'm not sure yet how I'd like to contribute.
(ASH turns and makes eye contact with WINNIE)
I'm sorry I don't think I caught your name...

WINNIE

I'm Winnie. I wanted to tell you that I grew up in the town you're from.

ASH

Oh, really? That's funny, it's such a small place. When did you move here?

WINNIE

Oh, I've been here a long time

now, thirty-two years. And I was
traveling before then, so it's
been a very long while since I've
lived there.

				JANE
	Winnie is a writer and artist,
	she makes good stuff.

				WINNIE
	Jane, come on! Don't embarrass
	me.

				ASH
	I'd love to see your work
	sometime.

				WINNIE
	Well, don't get too excited, but
	if you're not busy now I could
	show you some things I'm working
	on. My house isn't far from here,
	a little down the canal.

FADE OUT

						CUT TO

CANAL WALKWAY-NIGHT

Orange fish swim in the neon blue water, illuminated by streetlights. The sidewalk is mostly empty and WINNIE and ASH walk at a slow pace. The two are mid-conversation.

ASH

No, none of us had health insurance, so when my parents got that last round of virus we racked up a lot of debt from the hospital bills. That's partially why I moved here, when they passed away the bills transferred to my name, and back there there are no jobs. Here there is still some work at least.

WINNIE stops in front of a long blue boat floating in the canal.

WINNIE

I mean they preach prevention but they also fund all the production of the carcinogens and chemicals that are killing us and making our lives painful while we're still around... Ah here we are, this is my place!

WINNIE slowly reaches over and pulls back a tarp covering the deck.

ASH

You live here?

WINNIE

Yep, have had her since I moved to the city. It's the cheapest way to live here, and I like feeling

the water move under me while I
sleep. Can you help me down?

WINNIE motions to her arm, ASH grabs her and helps her step into the deck of the boat. WINNIE ducks through the door and ASH follows.

CUT TO

INTERIOR OF BOAT-DIM LIGHTING FROM LAMP-MUSIC PLAYING FROM RADIO

WINNIE and ASH are sitting at a table. The camera pans the room. The boat's ceilings are low, and it is full of dusty objects and drawings. There is stuff everywhere and the frame of the camera is continually rocking with the boat. They're drinking out of mugs. During the conversation the camera jumps cuts between close-ups of the speakers' faces.

                ASH
What are you working on right now?

              WINNIE
I have Multiple Sclerosis, and in the past few years whenever it flares up it's gotten really bad, so I'm writing a book about creating support systems for living with chronic disease. You met me on a good day, but some days I can't walk at all, I can't talk and I can barely

think. I don't have a partner, and, frankly, I haven't waited on or wanted one during my life. In this book I'm interviewing all kinds of people with different types of illness on how they ask for what they need from people in their life and how they make their own structures of survival inside of the current situation. I got into an insurance lottery a few years ago through Corp so I'm covered, thank god, but most people aren't, and anyway who knows how long that will last for me or any of us.

                    ASH
Is that how you got involved with the group?

                   WINNIE
Yes, I ended up interviewing someone who had been involved and they told me I should sit in on a meeting. You know the group used to be a patients' collective?

                    ASH
No, what's that?

                   WINNIE
Well, for us it was an alternative therapy group more focused on finding help with legal issues

surrounding insurance claims and getting aid to proceed through the court system. Basically collectivizing to deal with issues facing patients. However, it became clear recently that going through the motions legally was getting us nowhere, so we began to plan with more unconventional tactics for getting what we want.

ASH

Have you been a part of any of the actions?

WINNIE

Honey, you'd be surprised what a sick lady of my age can get away with. I would say it's criminal!
(Both laugh)
So, what do you like to do?

ASH

I draw or at least I used to before things got this stressful. I'm trying to find a construction job right now though.

WINNIE

Well, that shouldn't be hard. They're building all those towers in the middle of the city. I'd love to see your personal work sometime though. Oh, hey, why don't you come back here with me—

> I have some drawing materials you can have, my hands are too shaky for that these days...

FADE OUT

CUT TO

MEETING ROOM

A few weeks have passed. ASH is back in the meeting room sitting next to WINNIE. There is murmuring around the circle, which is smaller this time.

HEN is showing JANE something on a tablet screen.

> HEN
> I figured it out! We need a time window of only an hour or two to send prescriptions without getting noticed.

> JANE
> Okay, so that will happen at noon...

> WINNIE
> And then I'll enter Corp Medi-building to create a distraction.

> ASH
> I'll pick up Winnie around 12:30, she might be sedated. I have the medical record we prepared.

                    JANE
          This should leave a time window
          when we can send the prescriptions
          out from the database.

                    LORRAINE
          The rest of us should be here
          notifying recipients that they
          should pick up the prescriptions
          before the hack is detected.

The meeting begins to disperse. ASH and WINNIE are the last to leave as they prepare a fake medical record for WINNIE. ASH and WINNIE walk out together. WINNIE is struggling to walk, so ASH holds her up.

                    WINNIE
          What are you going to tell them
          when you try to get me out? That
          you're my daughter?

                    ASH
          (She smiles and a little awkwardly
          replies)
          I was thinking about telling them
          you're my lover.

                    WINNIE
          (Winks at ASH)
          Well then, you wanna walk me
          home?

FADE OUT

                                    CUT TO

INTERIOR OF BOAT-AFTERNOON LIGHT COMES THROUGH
GREEN CURTAINS

ASH and WINNIE are having sex. The camera shows this in a montage of close-ups of isolated body parts and skin. ASH makes WINNIE come, and then they lie down very still next to each other until their breathing slows. The camera pans out to show both of them.

The boat is rocking. ASH, who is still wearing her t-shirt, reaches beside the bed for her electronic cigarette and takes a drag. WINNIE'S hair spills across her pillow and bare breasts. They're both calm, and WINNIE is smiling wide, which is rare.

                    WINNIE
    You're helping me back away from
    the edge I was moving towards.

                    ASH
    The edge of what?

                    WINNIE
    Soft suffocating craziness? An old
    burning death-drive? Knowing this
    disease is going to kill me in the
    most painful ways very soon?... I
    don't know... I guess what I mean

             to say is you're giving me some
             excitement and joy, and it's been
             a fucking long time since I felt
             either of those.

There is a loud knock on the boat door. ASH
pulls on a shirt quickly.

                         WINNIE
             Hello? Who is it?
             (Gets up slowly while putting on
             a robe)

                         JANE
             Me!
             (She opens the door, speaking
             frantically)
             Have you guys seen what's going
             on the feeds right now?

                         ASH
             No, what's happening?

                         JANE
             I don't even know how to explain.

They sit back on the bed and look on Jane's
tablet at coverage of a press conference. The
camera focuses on the tablet. On screen a
person in a hospital gown is standing, staring
wide eyed into the camera, in front of about
twenty DRs with clipboards and lab coats.

                    NEWSCASTER
          Yes, what was thought impossible
          is possible. The first human clone,
          a masterpiece and triumph for the
          geneticists working at Corp*Plex.
          For now she is called CopyCat,
          but soon the DRs will give her a
          name and she will be integrated
          into the general population. We
          will continue coverage of this
          historic event throughout the
          coming weeks...

ASH, JANE and WINNIE continue to watch the
feed in stunned silence. The camera slowly
pans out from the boat to show a shot of the
canal and city lights in the distance.

FADE OUT

                                         CUT TO

APARTMENT INTERIOR-NIGHT

The group is having dinner at HEN'S apartment.
They crowd around a too-small table. The food
has been eaten and empty plates surround them.
The conversation is loud.

                    JANE
          We need to talk about the clone.
          Wait, Hen, did you sweep for bugs?

                    HEN
          Yeah, of course, before dinner.

Is Lorraine coming?

MAX
No, they messaged me, in too much pain tonight. I'll take them some leftovers after this.

WINNIE
I'll give them a call later to check in as well.

ASH
What do you all think of the clone?

HEN
I don't know what it means politically, but the idea of it gives me the creeps. . .

WINNIE
She did not choose to get into this mess.

ASH
Yeah I agree. I think it could be important to make contact. At least try to have her on our side.

JANE
Yes, I totally agree. Also we shouldn't forget that she is in the belly of the beast. She has access to Corp interior.

HEN
Did you hear they named her Prima?

MAX
Lord help her...How will we get her alone? She's surrounded by DRs and the press all the time.

ASH
Hen, could you find out where she works? The media says they're trying to "normalize" her as fast as possible, so she must have a job somewhere. Maybe we could find her there, probably less press, try to catch her in a bathroom or something when she's isolated to make contact?

HEN
I can try to figure that out.

WINNIE
Hell, she probably feels so lonely...and confused about all this. Maybe she'll be open to us.

JANE
We have to make sure however we talk to her that we won't scare her so she goes running to daddy. Corp is looking for us already and will be especially ruthless if they know we're trying to turn their precious project...

                    HEN
          Into a dropout freak?

                    MAX
     Queer?

                    WINNIE
     A weapon?

Laughter.

                    JANE
          Well, I was going to say an enemy
          of Corp...

FADE OUT

                                        CUT TO

INDUSTRIAL PARKING LOT-NIGHT

ASH'S feet framed in midair against the moon. The camera slowly pans out to show that she is in a dumpster in a corporate warehouse park, which stretches far into the distance. She is upside down searching for something. WINNIE stands beside the dumpster. The only noise that can be heard is the hum of the highway in the distance.

                    ASH
          I don't see anything, just
          garbage!
          (Climbs out of dumpster and picks

off some trash that has stuck to her)
Rumor or not, I mean, honestly any kind of free drugs are too good to be true.

WINNIE
There is one over there, want to check that one before we go?

ASH
Sure.
(Walks over to other dumpster and climbs in)
Holy shit.
(Starts throwing full pill bottles out)

WINNIE
(Picks up a bottle)
Holy hell, name brand too! We can really start our own pharmacy with all this!

ASH
You think these are defective?

WINNIE
No, probably overproduced or misprinted labels or something. You know these drugs don't even really go bad? At least for 30 years I've heard.

After ASH has emptied the dumpster, she loads the pill bottles into the car. They begin to drive back to the city. The camera frames both of their faces from the front, highlighted in the darkness by the flashes of light of other passing cars.

CAR-GLOW OF DASHBOARD

                    WINNIE
   Prima is in?

                    ASH
   As far as I can tell. Hen has
   been tracking her movement on
   the feeds and it looks like she
   is telling us the truth, hasn't
   outed us yet. She seems to want
   revenge even more than we do.

                    WINNIE
   Can you blame her?

                    ASH
   She told me that Corp is planning
   to mass produce a population of
   clones soon.

The weight of that information keeps ASH and WINNIE in silence for a minute. They both stare at the light of the city approaching through the window. After a while, ASH looks at the clock on the dashboard.

                    ASH
          It's late, let's drop these off
          with Jane and then I need to get
          some sleep for work tomorrow.

WINNIE puts her hand on ASH'S leg.

FADE OUT

                                              CUT TO

LARGE WAREHOUSE-NIGHT

ASH and JANE along with a few other members are
in a warehouse whispering to one another. The
camera moves quickly between the conversation.

                    JANE
          We have five minutes until Prima
          and Winnie do their part, and
          then we have a half hour before
          we have to get out of here.

                    HEN
          (Hen's voice coming through
          Jane's tablet)
          Cameras are down. Security down.

The group splits off quickly. ASH unloads boxes
labeled "VACCINES" onto a cart that Lorraine
is pushing. The camera follows LORRAINE as
they collect boxes from different members of
the group. The group moves, signaling to each
other with their hands but working in silence.
After the final box is loaded, the group gets

into the back of the truck. It drives away.

FADE OUT

CUT TO

BAR INTERIOR-NIGHT

ASH, JANE and WINNIE sit at a table in a crowded bar. The room is very silent and most everyone is watching the news playing from a tablet on the wall.

              NEWSCASTER
Breaking report, an unknown terrorist group is linked to three connected attacks this evening. The first at a pharma warehouse outside of the city center. Thousands of prescription drugs were stolen, the total value of the heist has not been calculated yet, but it is suspected to be in the millions. It is not known where or how the terrorists plan on selling these drugs. During this time, two bombs were also detonated. One in the Corp*Plex and another in the Medi-building. No one was hurt in these attacks. Both bombers set off the fire alarm before leaving the bombs to detonate, giving time for the buildings to be evacuated. The bombers

seemed to be targeting the modem rooms of each building where valuable information is stored for Corp. The culprit of Medi-building bombing has not been apprehended; however, we have recently received a report that the Corp*Plex bombing was done by Prima. She is in Corp custody now and further action is being decided upon by the geneticists and DRs.

Newscast cuts to a shot of a DR.

                  DR

We are terribly saddened and deeply disappointed by Prima's actions. Clearly this is an issue of hardwiring in her brain, so psychotherapy is our first course of action, as well as questioning to discover the identities of the other culprits. We will take this defiance and hysterical behavior as a warning sign which we will appropriately address in further clone formation. We are committed to creating law-abiding, productive and neurologically sound citizens.

                JANE

(In a whisper)
Holy shit.

WINNIE
She was ready to sacrifice herself, that was her own choice. We told her she didn't have to do that.

ASH
Jesus, Winnie, I mean still. Corp is going to kill her probably.

WINNIE
I know, I know. All I mean is that she knows what she is doing. She made a choice. Probably out of extreme anger, and honestly I don't blame her. I would be angry as hell too in her position. How are the drops going?

JANE
Hen is checking in with them. Everyone transporting them is responsible for destroying their barcodes, as long as that happens they can't really be tracked.

WINNIE
I think we all need a drink.

ASH
Let me get us another round.

FADE OUT

CUT TO

BOAT INTERIOR-EVENING

WINNIE and ASH are in WINNIE'S boat. They are sitting on WINNIE'S bed. A tablet is on quietly in the background playing the news. ASH has recently gotten off work and looks exhausted. The camera frames the two in conversation.

                    ASH
        When is the next meeting?

                  WINNIE
        I'm not sure. Let's take a break
        from that stuff though for one
        minute... I'm having a hard day,
        my brain feels foggy.

                  ASH
        Okay Win, it's fine. What do you
        want to do?

                  WINNIE
        Can you finally show me those
        drawings you've been working on?

                  ASH
        Sure.

ASH pulls out drawings from her bag. The camera is close up to the drawings so they fill the frame of the shot. The camera rests on each one to create a brief montage. She begins showing them to WINNIE. They are full of abstract lines and shapes, weaving forms—somewhere between DNA and lace—all in the same blue color of the canal.

WINNIE looks up to the tablet for a moment, and her expression changes to fear. ASH looks over from the drawings to realize what WINNIE is looking at.

> WINNIE
>
> Ash?

> ASH
> (Scrambles to turn up the volume)
> (On the screen is a blurry black and white pixelated image of ASH'S face in a hoodie from above)
> Shit.

> NEWSCASTER
> Prima has confirmed this is one of the suspected terrorists caught on a hidden security camera in the warehouse. The suspect's name is not known but facial recognition specialists are investigating. Tomorrow Prima will be making a public apology from Corp*Plex for her participation in the attacks. Please tune in at noon for this special livestream...

> ASH
> I thought all those cameras got disabled.

WINNIE sits down on the bed and closes her eyes tightly. The camera zooms into the television to show the image of ASH.

                    WINNIE
          (Speaking   slowly,   slightly
          shaking)
          We need to tell the group about
          this right away. If they've got
          Prima   talking,   we're   all   in
          danger.

FADE OUT

                                      CUT TO

JANE'S LIVING ROOM-EARLY MORNING

A larger group, maybe 30 people, sits in the
living room. The camera pans across the group.
Some are lying on the floor, some in chairs.
WINNIE is on the couch with her feet propped
up. A few people hold tablets of other members
videochatting into the meeting. Everyone
in the room has a worried expression. The
conversation is fast paced and loud.

                    LORRAINE
          Before we make any rash decisions
          we need to listen to her statement.

                    ASH
          Yeah, it's possible Corp has my
          picture and nothing else, and
          that they're lying that Prima is
          giving up information.

HEN

I knew we shouldn't have trusted her, look what's happening now!

WINNIE

(Angrily)
It's certainly not her fault they had that tape's footage. It was your job to make sure that didn't happen.

ASH

(Whispers to WINNIE angrily)
Win, stop it!

JANE

Well, not to cause more problems, but Ash did refuse to wear the anti-facial recognition makeup like I suggested...

ASH

Obviously now I feel completely ridiculous, but I hate wearing makeup, okay?

MAX

(Speaking from a tablet screen)
There are five minutes until the livestream. Can we all calm down until then? I can lead some breathing exercises if that will help.

The group murmurs in agreement. MAX begins counting off and the room is filled with the sound of breathing. Soon ASH rises and turns on a tablet. The camera zooms so it is close up to the tablet.

> NEWSCASTER
> Prima will shortly announce her apology from Corp*Plex. She has been under the intense supervision and questioning from DRs, psychologists, neurologists, psychoanalysts and law enforcement for the past two weeks.

News cuts to PRIMA who is standing behind a podium, her hands behind her back in zip-ties.

> PRIMA
> *Hello.*
>
> *Behind me, rebuilding has begun on the damaged structure.*
>
> *Today I am here to apologize for my actions.*
>
> *What I did was inexcusable, a terrible risk.*
>
> *Because of my position as the 1st clone,*
>
> *I must act more responsibly.*

I must be more compliant.

> *Corp says this is not anyone's fault it is a matter of language, also known as mismanaged code, which in the future will be rewritten into obedient clones. I am the warning bell.*

I do carry this weight. I did connect those wires to set off the explosion which led to the fire. I admit—

(Speaking faster, gripping microphone)

in the short time I have been alive

> *I owe everything I know to Corp, namely, this body.*

> *But if my body was made well; under the most idyllic, hygienic, and empirical conditions,*

> *why do I feel so unwell?*

A tireless cycle:

> *failing bodies in precarious situations asking for assistance.*
>
> *They claim they will, through their technology, and by leveraging your free will:*
>> *heal you.*
>
> *However, their investors and political allies poison the entire population through physical and bureaucratic conditions making us dependent on their medical attention. Your bodies are*
>> *capital investment while they act as if your pain and death are simply collateral damage that cannot be helped.*

The broadcast is abruptly interrupted by a commercial break.

CUT TO

FADE IN

CORP*PLEX-MIDDAY

PRIMA is still in front of Corp, struggling against security guards who are trying to stop her from speaking to the crowd that has gathered in front of her. She continues to yell.

PRIMA
Do you even realize your flesh and organs' literal worth? You are bloody goldmines, friends.

And I hate to be the one to tell you this but...

> *But a large majority of current suffering comes from a repetitive pattern that started long ago.*

Like,

this has all been happening for centuries. The real healers were killed off one by one and no one stopped the series of exterminations, just let them all burn and burn and let all the knowledge burn too.

So,

no wonder all the ill are now called broken and there is a notion of being fixed in singular correct means.

> *No wonder I am obsessed with identifying the point of breakage.*

I broke this—

(Flings arms towards the burnt building behind her)

because I'm broken and all I know to do is break.

PRIMA is tackled to the ground by security and held down while the DRs speak behind her in a mass deciding how to proceed. At this point no one can hear her talking, but she continues her speech with her mouth pressed against the ground. The camera zooms in closer to her face, the viewer is able to see her sweating slightly from her upper lip, her eyes piercing. Her sound muffled but audible.

>PRIMA
>*Someone named me a few months ago, a name which, as of now,*
>
>*I publically refuse.*
>
>*Call me Miss Judgment instead.*
>*Call me Miss Fit*
>*Miss Take*
>*Miss Led*
>*Miss Interpret*
>*Miss Made*
>*or better yet,*
>*Miss Copy.*

> *Locked in my room I used my*
> *fingernails to cut open my*
> *skin until I bled*

just to know
I'm real and
not a poorly
constructed

missing link or monster or
scientific savior or sick son of a
bitch, or any of the other titles I
have heard others call me during my
short life.

> *Did any of you really come*
> *here today*
> > *for empathy*
> > > *tangible facts*
> > > > *To witness*
> > > > *a truth?*

or just spectacle?

I am...

A DR approaches PRIMA from above and plunges a tranquilizer into her neck. She immediately goes limp and her words cut off.

CUT TO

FADE IN

JANE'S LIVING ROOM-MIDDAY

The group continues to sit in stunned silence. HEN gets up and turns the tablet off. Many in the room are crying. A few members get up wordlessly and leave to the kitchen. JANE is breathing quickly on the ground, and LORRAINE moves over to quell her panic attack. HEN is the first to break the silence. The camera moves to center her face, the others still visible in the background.

                    HEN
    We've got to get her out of there.

                   END

EPILOGUE

Dear reader,

This book was written on the slowly compounded rage of navigating the medical industrial pharmaceutical system for the past ten years of my life. It was a response to my allopathic doctors saying that I would be crazy to try to not take medication for my chronic disease, or multiple doctors simply calling me crazy and suggesting I should get evaluated for an anxiety disorder instead of listening to my needs. It was written for the struggle to be insured with a pre-existing condition as a teenager. It was a means to articulate my desire for an insurrectionary politics that was centered and embedded around care, organized and catalyzed from those called "ill."

I began this book in the winter of 2015 after finishing undergrad. I was feeling lost and frustrated navigating a series of bad doctors and the floating dread of having an invisible illness within the precarity of working and living in New York City. Since then many things have shifted for me personally as well as politically. I feel blessed that my path has brought me to seeking alternative health practitioners and organizing around these issues with others and in community, both of which have directed my energies (all of it—the rage, sadness, but also deep joy) towards more connectedness and webs of life building that make me (the sick me, the exhausted me, the dancing me—all my multiples) feel more possible.

Publishing this after the election of Trump was confusing in many ways. Through the editing process I faced a lot of self-doubt that the world I was proposing in the text I could no longer completely stand with. I recently read

Marge Piercy's amazing novel *Woman on the Edge of Time* (go, read this!), and in my journal I wrote *i am deeply tired of writing about dystopias. world build towards a means of collective living you desire. there is too much at stake right now.*

I am putting this into the world with a grain of salt. Presently I want to begin to write a different world, a spell for a more caring one, and the imagined excitement, mess and living that place could propose.

For now I hope this book can speak through the fiction to resonate with backgrounds both similar and different from mine. I hope it resonates with any who have had traumatic experiences with doctors. To those with diagnosis or not. To those who deal with pain on a daily, monthly, yearly basis, or who are stuck in the psychological state of waiting for chronic pain to someday return. If anything I hope this book deals with the fact that even as a patient there can be an feeling of empowerment through the connection to others with the shared experience of being described as unwell, crazy or physically or mentally dysfunctional. That at some point we will all be sick, feel pain and discomfort, and I believe that this intersectional moment is a place to begin organizing from and towards alternative ideas of health, disability justice and care in relation to our bodies, ability and the health of the planet we all inhabit.

WITH CARE AND BLESSINGS.

BIBLIOGRAPHY

This work came from research and reading about the medical industrial complex and historical movements that center radical healthcare. Since writing this, I have found and befriended groups and individuals working on this subject that are researching and practicing alternative models of care. I include their work as well.

Ehrenreich, Barbara; English, Deirdre. *Witches, Midwives, and Nurses: A History of Women Healers*. Old Westbury, N.Y: Feminist Press, 1973. Print.

Federici, Silvia. *Caliban and the Witch: Women, the Body and Primitive Accumulation*. New York: Autonomedia, 2003.

Feministische Gesundheitsrecherchegruppe / Feminist Health Care Research Group. *Being in Crisis Together Zine #3*, Berlin. 2017. For their work see, http://www.feministische-recherchegruppe.org/

Hedva, Johanna. "Sick Woman Theory." *Mask Magazine*. Web. Jan. 16, 2016.

Jane Collective Abortion Service Archive, http://www.cwluherstory.org/Jane-Abortion-Service/

Kapil, Bhanu. *Incubation: a space for monsters*. Leon Works, 2006.

Lazard, Carolyn. " How to Be a Person in the Age of Autoimmunity." *The Cluster Mag*. January 16, 2013.

Lorde, Audre. *The Cancer Journals*. Special ed. San Francisco: Aunt Lute Books, 1997.

"On The History Of The Use Of Acupuncture By Revolutionary Health Workers To Treat Drug Addiction, And US Government Attacks Under The Cover Of The CounterIntelligence Program (COINTELPRO)." *Mutulu Shakur : stiff ahead, straight resistance*. https://www.mutulushakur.com/interview-lompoc.html/

Power Makes us Sick (PMS). *Zines Issue #1 & #2*. 2017. Print. For their work see, https://pms.hotglue.me/

Rankine, Claudia. *Don't Let Me Be Lonely: An American Lyric*. Saint Paul, Minn: Graywolf Press, 2004. Print.

SPK - *Turn Illness Into A Weapon*, self-published translation, 1993.

ACKNOWLEDGEMENTS

Thank you Ruth Pilston for your careful reading and Arcadia Missa for publishing the second edition of this text. Love and RIP to Monster House Press, thank you to all who were apart of that beautiful project and for believing in my work.

For the loves, friends, comrades, caretakers and word witches in my life that helped me practically, energetically and emotionally through the writing process; Tori Abernathy, Ernest Ah, Moriah Askenaizer, Jakob Beirnat, Bella Bravo, Anke Brucker, L Electricity, Isabel Gatzke, Caspar Jade Heinemann, Constanza Hermosilla, Alice Sparkly Kat, Jordan Martin, Sasha P, Saar Shemesh, Emmanuela Soria Ruiz, Sara Swan, Alex Velozo, Anna-Irini Vila, Tine Völcker, Romily Alice Walden, Richard Wehrenberg, Inga Zimprich, and Sickness Affinity Group Berlin. Thank you for the editing, conversations, spiritual holding and for pushing me to share.

I feel indebted and grateful for those in my life living with chronic illness, your ingrained and embodied wisdom has taught me so much.

Bless and learned bureaucratic fortitude from my mother, who sat on hold and in argument with insurance companies for too many hours of her life. To both of my parents for taking care of me during diagnosis and uncertainty when I was young.

Thanks to my grandmother, Ann Dudley Matheny. For your encouragement and stories, love of words and writing, and uncompromising joy and excitement for the world.

Gratitude to my big teachers, the ocean, trees, obsidian, red clover.

ABOUT THE AUTHOR

Clay AD makes and thinks collectively and individually around themes of sci-fi, illness, holistic healing and ecology and they offer their work to you. Born in Indianapolis, Indiana and now living in Berlin, AD studies somatic bodywork and movement. *Metabolize, If Able* was named a finalist in the 31st annual Lambda Literary Award for LGBTQ Sci-Fi, Fantasy and Horror.